My Class Decides Together

CIVIC VIRTUES

Naomi Wells

CiViCS FOR THE REAL WORLD™

Rosen Classroom™

Published in 2019 by The Rosen Publishing Group, Inc.
29 East 21st Street, New York, NY 10010

Book Design: Haley Robinson
Editor: Ryan Wolf

Photo Credits: Cover, p. 4, 7, 8, 12, 14 Rawpixel.com/Shutterstock.com; p. 11 hxdbzxy/Shutterstock.com.

ISBN: 9781538365052
6-pack ISBN: 9781538365069

Manufactured in the United States of America

CPSIA Compliance Information: Batch #WS18RC: For Further Information contact Rosen Publishing, New York, New York at 1-800-237-9932

Table of Contents

In the Classroom

There are many different kinds of people in the world. People have different backgrounds. They like different things. They have different **opinions**. Your classroom at school may have many different kinds of people, too. But you all have your class in common.

Decisions to Make

Sometimes your class may need to make decisions about something at school. Maybe you need to decide what to do for a **project**. Maybe you need to name a class pet. Perhaps you need to choose how to decorate your classroom.

Different Opinions

Different people will have different opinions on the decision. Some of them may feel very strongly about the choices. It's important to stay calm and respect others' opinions. Listen to them and ask them to listen to you.

Ways to Decide

There are different ways to make a decision as a class. You could take a vote. You could **appoint** one trusted person to make a decision. You could also talk about it. See if there's an **option** everyone can agree on.

What Works Best?

It's important to think carefully about decisions before you make them. You can't always change your mind later! Consider what works best. Think about why other people feel the way they do. Try to make an **informed** choice.

It's Decided!

If you and your classmates think things through, you can make a good decision together. It's important to listen and be informed. That will help you make the best decisions you can, for yourself and for your classroom.

Glossary

appoint: To name someone to do something.

informed: Having information, or facts about something.

opinion: A belief or way of thinking about something.

option: Something that can be chosen.

project: A task or problem for learning.

Index